To J., G., A., and H.
—T. S.

For Zénaïde
—R. B.

Henry Holt and Company, LLC
Publishers since 1866
175 Fifth Avenue, New York, New York 10010
mackids.com

Library of Congress Cataloging-in-Publication Data
Names: Sloat, Teri, author. | Bonnet, Rosalinde, illustrator.
Title: Pablo in the snow / Teri Sloat ; illustrated by Rosalinde Bonnet.
Description: First edition. | New York : Henry Holt and Company, 2017. |
Summary: "The heartwarming tale of one little lamb's first snowy adventure" —Provided by publisher.
Identifiers: LCCN 2016002103 | ISBN 9781627794121 (hardback)
Subjects: | CYAC: Sheep—Fiction. | Snow—Fiction. |
BISAC: JUVENILE FICTION / Concepts / Seasons. | JUVENILE FICTION / Animals / Farm Animals.
Classification: LCC PZ7.1.S5915 Pab 2017 | DDC [E]—dc23
LC record available at https://lccn.loc.gov/2016002103

Our books may be purchased in bulk for promotional, educational, or business use.
Please contact your local bookseller or the Macmillan Corporate and Premium Sales Department at
(800) 221-7945 ext. 5442 or by e-mail at MacmillanSpecialMarkets@macmillan.com.

First Edition—2017 / Designed by Patrick Collins
The illustrations for this book were made with India ink and watercolor
on 165-lb. Clairefontaine paper and finalized in Adobe Photoshop.
Printed in China by Toppan Leefung Printing Ltd., Dongguan City, Guangdong Province

1 3 5 7 9 10 8 6 4 2

Pablo
in the Snow

TERI SLOAT

illustrated by ROSALINDE BONNET

Christy Ottaviano Books
Henry Holt and Company ✦ New York

It's early in the morning and the sheep are still dreaming.

Except for Pablo.

Pablo is looking out the window.

"Look, Papa! Pieces of clouds are falling!"

Papa opens one eye. "Those are just snowflakes, Pablo. Go back to sleep."

But Pablo has never seen snow. "What is it for?" he wonders.

He tiptoes past his papa and his mama to the barn door.

Pablo pokes the snow with his toe.

The snow feels soft, powdery, and fluffy.

He takes a few steps and looks at the tracks behind him.

"Snow is for making a trail," says Pablo.

But who has made this trail?

Pablo follows long tracks until
he finds Rabbit pulling her sled.

"Hop on!" says Rabbit.

Zip, zoom, swoosh, swish!

They ride through the trees and into the meadow.

"Snow is for fun!" shouts Pablo.

At the bottom of the hill, Pablo finds new tracks to follow.

Something sails past Pablo's nose.

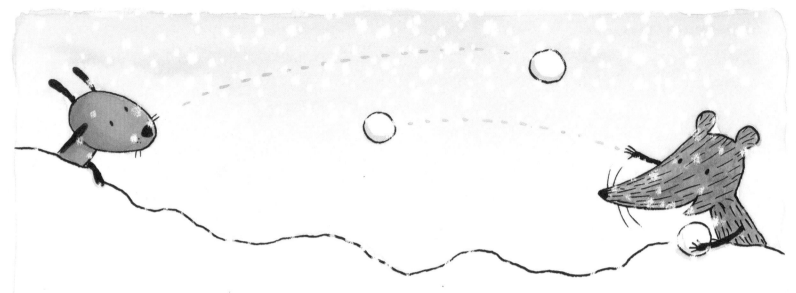

Squirrel and Shrew are having a snowball fight.

Back and forth, snowballs fly.

"Snow is for throwing!"

shouts Pablo, ducking his head.

Pablo finds more tracks.

They lead him to the other side of the meadow,
where Fox is rolling a big snowball.

But instead of throwing it,
he rolls it bigger and bigger.

The snowball grows round
and smooth and heavy.

Pablo helps Fox roll a second, bigger snowball.

And then a third one.

With Rabbit's help, they stack the snowballs one on top of the other.

Squirrel finds an acorn for the nose.

Rabbit places frozen berries into a big smile.

Pablo reaches up with two flat, round stones for the eyes.

And, with Fox's help, Shrew adds a warm, fuzzy scarf.

"Snow is for making friends," says Pablo, laughing.

The snow is falling faster now.

"It's time to go back to my den," says Fox.

Squirrel scurries up his tree.

Shrew and Rabbit disappear into their burrows.

But Pablo does not want
to leave his snowy friend behind.

He looks up at the sky.

Thick, gray snowflakes fall quietly.

Pablo's friend looks very sleepy.

Pablo feels sleepy, too.

"Good night," Pablo tells his snow friend. "Sleep tight."

The snow is deep and wet and cold.

I need to go home, thinks Pablo.

Pablo looks for his tracks,

but they have disappeared.

Pablo is lost.

"Baaaaa!" says Pablo.

Through the trees, Pablo hears,

"Baaa! Baaaa!"

Pablo knows these sounds.

At the edge of the trees,

he sees two lumps of snow . . .

with legs.

One lump has Mama's eyes. One lump has Papa's eyes.

Both lumps say, "Baaaaa!" and give Pablo a big kiss.

Together they make a
trail back to the barn.

They shake off the snow
and snuggle close in the straw.

"Snow is for big adventures," thinks Pablo.
"But snow is cold, and the barn is warm and dry,
and Mama and Papa are very, very cozy."